For Mum and Kim, forever in my thoughts — D.K.

To all the dogs ever, big and small — L.X.

Text © 2019 Deborah Kerbel | Illustrations © 2019 Lis Xu

Owlkids Books acknowledges the financial support of the Canada Council for the Arts,
the Ontario Arts Council, the Government of Canada through the Canada Book Fund (CBF)
and the Government of Ontario through the Ontario Creates Book Initiative
for our publishing activities.

Published in Canada by Owlkids Books Inc., 1 Eglinton Avenue East, Toronto, ON M4P 3A1
Published in the US by Owlkids Books Inc., 1700 Fourth Street, Berkeley, CA 94710

Library of Congress Control Number: 2018963954

Library and Archives Canada Cataloguing in Publication

Kerbel, Deborah, author
When Molly drew dogs / written by Deborah Kerbel
; illustrated by Lis Xu.

ISBN 978-1-77147-338-5 (hardcover)

I. Xu, Lis, illustrator II. Title.

PS8621.E75W54 2019   jC813'.6   C2018-906512-5

Edited by Karen Li | Designed by Alisa Baldwin

Manufactured in Shenzhen, Guangdong, China, in March 2019, by WKT Co. Ltd.
Job #18CB3393

A   B   C   D   E   F

ONTARIO ARTS COUNCIL
CONSEIL DES ARTS DE L'ONTARIO
an Ontario government agency
un organisme du gouvernement de l'Ontario

Canada Council   Conseil des Arts
for the Arts   du Canada

Canadä

Owl kids
Publisher of Chirp, Chickadee and OWL
www.owlkidsbooks.com | Owlkids Books is a division of   bayard canada

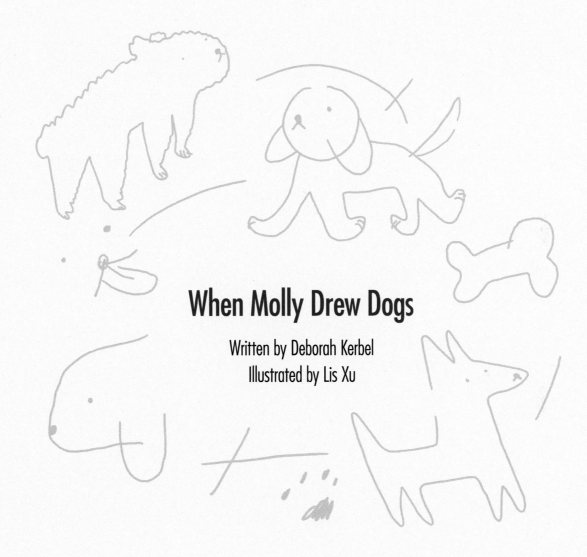

When Molly Drew Dogs

Written by Deborah Kerbel
Illustrated by Lis Xu

Owlkids Books

On the night before the first day of
school, a pack of stray dogs moved
into Molly Akita's head.

They were friendly. But a bit wild.

They scampered through her thoughts. And yapped at the door to her dreams.

When they got restless, they scratched at her brain, begging to be let out.

So Molly started
drawing them …

... everywhere.

When Molly drew dogs, her heart sat up and smiled.

Not everyone felt
the same way.

Molly's new teacher, Ms. Shepherd, must have been allergic to dogs.

"It's time to get serious, Molly."

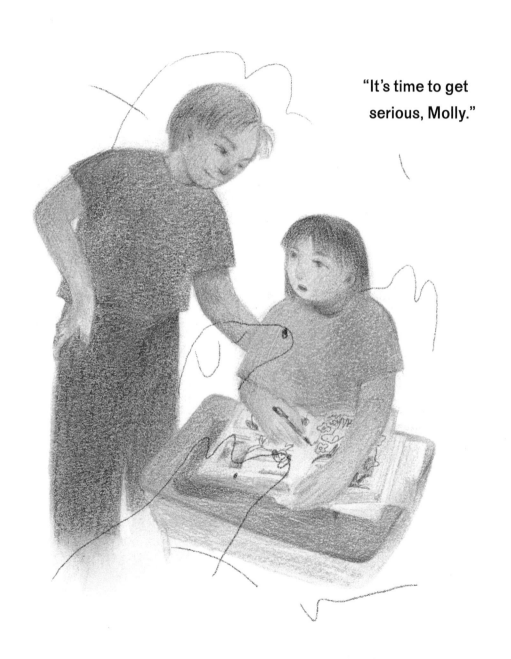

"Focus on your work."

"Drawing is only
for art class."

But Molly's dogs were
stubborn. They needed
to run free.

A letter was sent home
to Grandma.

The next evening after work, Grandma brought Molly to see a tutor.

"Mr. Russell teaches children how to concentrate on their schoolwork," she said. "Be a good girl and pay attention."

Molly tried. She really did. But her dogs just wouldn't sit still.

Halfway through the lesson, Mr. Russell lost his patience.

"No dogs allowed!"

Molly turned tail and ran. Her dogs were causing so much trouble. But she couldn't erase them, even if she wanted to.

She ran and ran, until a pattering of raindrops brought her to a stop.
Wiping her eyes, she looked around. There was just enough light for
her to see that she was lost.

As the clouds opened up, she ducked inside a garden shed, the closest shelter she could find.

It was scary out in the world all by herself. Molly pulled out her chalk.

She gave the littlest dog a coat because he would be chilly on a night like this. Then she drew coats for the rest in case they were cold, too.

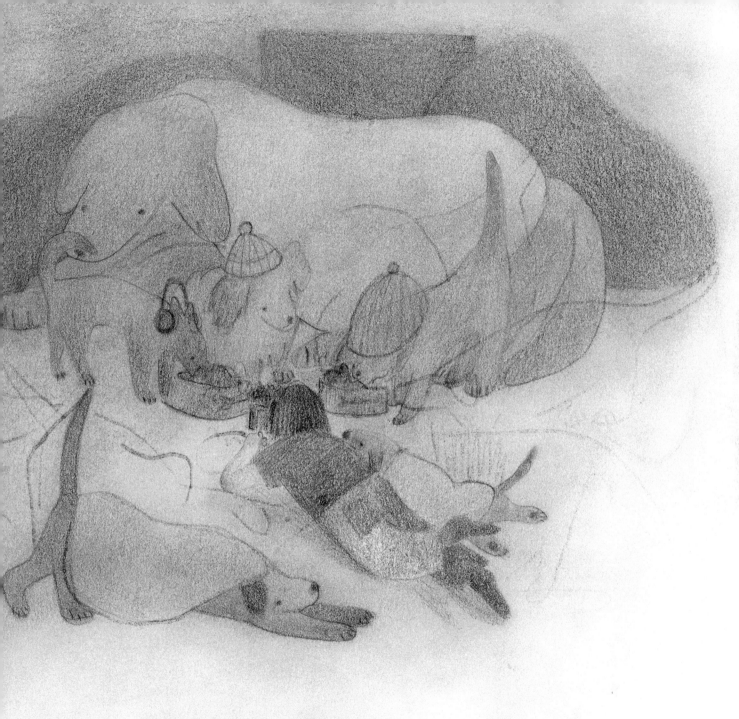

She drew bowls of food because they were probably very hungry.
Her stomach whined in sympathy.

Surrounded by a pack of friendly faces, Molly fell asleep.

Molly startled awake to the sound of barking and growling outside the shed.
It was too dark to see anything. She was too afraid to move.

Suddenly, there was an earsplitting howl. And then silence.

Molly curled up into a ball in the
far corner of the shed and wished,
wished, wished for morning.

In the fuzzy light of dawn, a face appeared at the door.

"Molly! We've been looking everywhere for you!"

"I … I heard barking. And howling. What happened?"

"There was a robber in the neighborhood last night.
But a pack of dogs scared him off. A pack of dogs …
wearing coats."

Molly turned toward her drawings
from the night before.

Ms. Shepherd stared at the dogs for a long time. Then she stared at Molly for even longer.

Finally, she held out her hand.

"Let's get you home."

As it turned out, Ms. Shepherd wasn't allergic to dogs after all.